Broken: A Billionaire Boys novel
By Henley Maverick

Chapter 1
Dixie

Time was suspended, warping all around her, the conversation distorted, people moving all around her were nothing but a blur, a blip on her radar. She was underwater, with everything muffled.

Except for *him*.

He was as clear and vivid as stars sprinkled across the night sky, bright and alluring, and she couldn't take her eyes away from him. In fact, a part of her felt like it was all surreal, some kind of daydream brought on by one too many glasses of wine.

Liquid courage rearing its ugly ahead.

Yet, he seemed real enough, or at least the reaction on his face indicated that, throwing her for a loop, back in time to five years ago when he had an eerily similar look on his face.

He hadn't changed one bit, not as far as she was concerned.

If anything, he was far better looking than she remembered, her mind having distorted her image to protect her from the truth, the ugly break up. Years of studying to be a lawyer and taking part in small cases should've prepared her for anything even remotely confrontational, allowing her to channel her inner Viola Davis, but instead she found that words eluded her.

Floating up in whispered tendrils of smoke before they vanished, leaving nothing behind, but her thoughts swirling round and round, compounding till she felt she was about to burst.

Maybe she shouldn't have walked over to him after all.

Truthfully, she had no idea why she was even standing there, bucking up the courage to talk to him, especially in light of the way things ended, a dark cloud hanging over both their heads.

Yet, she'd been sitting there, out of all the pubs in San Francisco, and there weren't very many, nursing a dirty martini, and pressing her fingers to her temples, trying to rid herself of the incredibly long day she had when she heard his voice.

Yes, she would recognize it anywhere, the gruff texture of it, honey sliding against her skin. At first, she'd been convinced it was her mind playing tricks on her because the odds that he was in the same place as her at the same time were slim, a needle in a haystack really.

She'd kept her eyes fixed on her drink, her plate of food forgotten next to her, growing colder by the minute, afraid to look up and have visual confirmation. In spite of her better judgment, she'd glanced up and sucked in a harsh breath, her eyes fixed on Aiden sitting there, mid laugh, his mouth full of food.

Shit.

He looked *good*, better than good actually; he looked *great*, his tan skin had a healthy glow to it, sun kissed, and his piercing blue eyes twinkled with mischief, lips curved into a half smile as he shot the man with him a dirty look.

Her heart did an odd little stutter, suspended in time, and just like that five years melted away, as if they hadn't happened. The rest of the room faded, vague silhouettes and outlines of color, whizzing past.

Abruptly, she'd stood up, downed the rest of her drink and walked over, running her hands over the pencil skirt and blouse, as nervous as she was the first day she spoke to him, a teenager riddled with butterflies.

"Aiden," Dixie greeted, offering him a small albeit forced smile. "How are you?"

Aiden was staring at her like his own personal ghost had come back to haunt him, in the flesh. His fingers drew forward before they curled in, and he hastily snatched his hand way, hoping she hadn't noticed.

He swallowed, his face pale, and his mouth pressed into a thin tight line.

Standing in front of him, she could hardly believe five whole years had passed since she laid eyes on him, remnants of their last conversation reverberating in her mind, a broken record on repeat.

No, it hadn't been an amicable breakup, not even close, but enough time had passed that she hoped his wounds had healed, scabbing over and fading away till they were nothing but a faint memory; a phantom limb that acted up every so often.

Judging by the look on his face, she had to guess that it wasn't the case.

There was a soft undercurrent of anger lurking in his eyes mixed in with a sense of confusion, yet he still remained obstinately quiet, refusing to acknowledge her existence aside from sputtering her name, choking it out like it was poison.

His mouth had struggled to form the words, and she knew why.

Dixie cleared her throat and turned her attention to his friend whose gaze was swinging back and forth between the two of them, eyebrows knitted together.

"Hi. It's nice to meet you, I'm sure. Would it be okay if I borrowed Aiden for a few minutes?"

The man gave a start of surprise, his dark eyes uncertain before he shrugged. "Yeah, sure."

This wasn't exactly a conversation she looked forward to having, not in the slightest, but Aiden needed to know the truth, and she'd spent years visualizing the moment, how they would both look and feel, the passage of time having softened the blow.

Now, she wished it was under better circumstances, but facts remained facts, and he needed to know that Dixie was back, to get over the shock, a jolt going through his entire central system, so he could adjust and prepare accordingly.

After all, they were supposed to face each other in court, and she would rather they clear the air, dispel any echoes of ill tidings before they got to the nitty gritty of it, the professional façade they would be expected to keep up as lawyers on opposing teams.

She doubted Aiden would be thrilled with the news; in fact, she could already see a slight muscle ticking in his jaw, annoyed at being forced into a corner, with his back against the wall, but she knew that this needed to be over and done with.

For the sake of their clients, both of them needed to get past their history, and put their best foot forward. At the end of the day, they were in the business of defending people, and while sometimes the crimes were petty, this was not the case here.

Frankie DeCeasare was being charged with murder, first degree to be exact, and she knew that as the DA, Aiden was dead set on putting him away, locking him up and throwing away the key so to speak.

Granted, the evidence against her client was mounting, and a lot of it was troubling. Why, she had to stay up late most nights just to find a shred of doubt to plant in the minds of jury, just a sliver was enough to get Frankie off with either a lesser sentence or a complete acquittal.

So far, she had her job cut out for her.

The only thing she knew for certain was that her client was being framed, this she believed without a shadow of a doubt, not only because the evidence seemed haphazard and random, a second grade project thrown together, but also because she knew the victim personally.

Frankie was a friend of her brother's, and ultimately, it was the reason she agreed to the case to begin with. Usually, she stayed away from any cases with personal ties, not wanting to get sucked into that particular vortex.

Since Frankie was only a family friend and not a blood relative, there was no rule against taking up his case, but she knew that her brother would bust her ass if she didn't manage to get them a home run, or at the very least, no jail time.

Luckily for him, the case appealed to her, and she'd agreed to take it on pro bono even though it meant flying back out to San Francisco, the city she left behind, a vague memory in her rearview mirror.

Being back wasn't easy for a number of reasons, the most prominent of which was sitting right in front of her, gaping as if she hadn't asked for a few minutes of his time but instead had asked for a blood sacrifice.

Yes, she should've anticipated this wouldn't be easy, not only because of Aiden's involvement, but because she knew how he felt about murder cases, if there was even a kernel of doubt, he was like a Pitbull, refusing to relinquish his hold until he had what he wanted.

Realistically, Dixie knew it wasn't a good idea for her to get involved, especially when she made the rookie mistake of looking at the client's innocence rather than the evidence. It was one of the first rules she taught herself; never question whether or not a client truly did it.

It had served her well so far.

Granted, she never had a client being framed for murder, her conscience nibbling away at her, demanding that she get to the bottom of things, but she trusted her instinct, her sixth sense, and she was going to see this through till the end.

Regardless of who opposed her.

Finally, Aiden gave his head a slight shake, disbelief written all over his features before he pushed his chair back, the loud scrape echoing back to them, drawing a few curious looks from the other people at the pub before they turned their attention away and back to their drinks.

Aiden shot his friend a long look, full of hidden tent before he gestured for her to lead the way, his eyes narrowed into slits. Dixie squared her shoulders and took two steps forward, making a beeline for the quiet corner in the back which was currently unoccupied.

An ideal place to have this conversation, or at least as good as it was going to get all things considered. She didn't expect the rolled out welcome wagon, or a marching band to hail her return, but she hoped to get two words in edgewise before Aiden went off.

And he most definitely would.

She glanced back, noticed the tense set of his jaw, and the way his hands clenched into fists at his side. He was a dormant volcano, ready to burst at the slightest provocation, and Dixie wasn't going to get away from the damage.

In fact, she was likely to be the debris when he was through.

Someone jostled past her, and she paused, rubbing her shoulders while Aiden caught up to her and brushed past, zeroing in on the corner she had her eyes on. It was exactly teen feet away from his table.

At the end of the day, she doubted Aiden would cause a scene somewhere public. Granted, he was prone to outbursts, a stream of emotions bursting forth, but he was able to keep a tight lid on it in public, believing that arguments were meant to be kept private.

And she would say this, although Aiden had the tendency to fly off the handle, he'd never once crossed the line and done something unforgivable. To his credit, she could say with absolute conviction.

Towards the end, their relationship had been fraught with problems, a revolving door of them, but he had never mistreated her the entire time, even when she had wronged him.

No, Dixie was under no illusions regarding whose fault it is.

In fact, she accepted responsibility for her actions, wholly and completely, and would even get down on her knees and offer herself up if she thought it would make things better, but it wouldn't.

She couldn't change the past any more than she could make Aiden less angry.

Besides, she was a different person back then, and she couldn't alter the hand she'd been dealt. Right now, the best she could do was deal with it, with as much pride and grace as possible.

Exactly teen feet away, Aiden whirled around and pinned her with a deadly look.

"*What the hell are you doing here?*" he hissed, not bothering to keep the fury out of his tone.

Chapter 2
Aiden

A part of him wondered if maybe he had a little bit too much to drink. It was entirely possible that with Julian's unusual engagement news, he had one too many because this had to be some kind of vivid hallucination.

There was no fucking way this was real.

He just refused to believe it.

He'd met up with Julian, knocked back a few strong drinks, and somehow managed to hit his head and end up in alternate world where the woman he once thought was the love of his life was asking him if they could talk.

Converse.

He scrubbed his hands over his face and resisted the urge to pinch himself, the strong smell of booze, and the steady thump of music over the speakers enough of an indication that he was in fact, very much, awake.

Though he wished with every fiber of his being that he wasn't.

Dixie fucking Aricello.

She was standing close enough for him to reach out and touch her shoulder, feeling the steady thrum of her heart beneath his fingertips, an indication that she was here too, not just a figment of his imagination.

Fuck.

She looked so much better than he remembered, with her pencil skirt, and button down blouse with the first one undone, showing off a hint of tanned skin. Right now, she was peering up at him, her brown eyes appraising and slightly wary, not that he could blame her.

In this scenario, she might as well have been walking into the lion's den, with her being the pray, and him being the roaring lion, angry and in pain. After what she did to him, he had every right to be, and no one could tell otherwise.

He didn't care that five years had come and gone, in the blink of an eye, like he'd the fast forward on a remote. As far as he was concerned, he was thrust back in time, unceremoniously, and it was just the two of them once more, facing each other like nothing else mattered.

Except it did.

Everything else did.

Five years ago, there was nothing he wouldn't have done for the woman in front of him, bent over backwards, gone to the ends of the Earth and back just to see her laugh, and he would've done it gladly.

Now, he couldn't even remember why.

After all, *she* was the one who left *him*. The memory of that was seared into his brain, etched into his DNA for as long as he drew breath, and he didn't think he'd ever be able to forget the way she looked, sadness weighing heavily on her, or the weight that had settled around his heart, an anchor dragging him down.

Yes, the memory was much too real for him, the pain echoing softly, even now. Five years, one thousand eight hundred and twenty five days later, and his heart still fluttered around her, the traitorous organ skipping around in his chest.

In spite of what she did to him, the way she left him in shambles, a complete mess, and a shell of his former self, he couldn't deny that it was good to see her; her beauty still managed to knock the breath out of him.

Angrily, he shoved the nostalgia away, refusing to let it blur the edges, softening the blow of what she did. He balled his hands into his fists, and wheeled around, barely able to bit his tongue any longer.

Out of respect for Julian, and his aversion to creating a scene, he'd refused to comment or even dignify her request with a response, preferring to let the silence do the talking, but he couldn't hold it back any longer, the damn threatening to burst.

"*What the hell are you doing here?*" he hissed, fury coating his tone.

Dixie blinked. "It's a pub. Am I not allowed to have a drink?"

"Don't you dare," Aiden replied, voice dripping with acid. "This is not the time for a smart ass comment, Dixie, and you know it."

Dixie sighed, but said nothing.

"Look, I don't know what the hell you're doing back here, and frankly, I'm not even sure I care, but you can't just waltz back into my life like we're old pals or something."

"Why can't we be?" Dixie asked, calmly.

Aiden raised an eyebrow and crossed his arms over his chest. "Are you fucking kidding me? Do you want a play by play of the last time we saw each other? Shall I reenact it for you?"

Dixie shook her head. "No, there's no need for that."

"No need?" Aiden repeated. "No shit, Sherlock. Aren't you observant? After all this time, what gives you the right to be standing here? Acting like nothing happened?"

To her credit, Dixie didn't flinch, didn't even look perturbed in the face of his wrath. However, it was likely because she'd prepped herself for the inevitability; Dixie was the type of person who liked to prepare for everything.

This was probably no exception.

"I'm not acting like nothing happened," Dixie disagreed, a slight tremor in her voice. "I just choose not to let it affect my current actions."

Aiden scoffed. "Spoken like a true lawyer, *counselor*."

"Speak for yourself, Mr. DA," Dixie retorted. "Look, I didn't come here to hash out the past or for some kind of confrontation."

Aiden frowned. "No? Because you excel in that particular area, you know. I should know. You're an expert when it comes to twisting and warping the truth, so you come out looking like the victim."

"That's not true."

"Yes, it is," Aiden retorted, coldly. "You betrayed me, Dixie. There's no way to spin that story, not even if you wanted to, and you're welcome to try, God knows I certainly have, but regardless of how you frame it, the end result is the same."

Dixie's mouth slammed shut, and she looked ashamed, shifting her eyes elsewhere as she shifted from one foot to the other, recognizing the truth in his words.

"I know I did," Dixie admitted, softly, her eyes still cast downward. "But I thought that enough time had passed by now."

Aiden's eyes narrowed further. "Enough time passed for what? To waltz back into my life and turn it upside down? You leaving destroyed *me*, Dixie. You and I both know that, so I'm not going to mince words. You're *not* welcome here, nor do I have *any* interest in you coming into my life after all this time looking to make amends. It's too *late*."

Deep down, Aiden didn't actually believe that, or at least his heart didn't, and it did an odd little lurch at his choice of words, sulking and refusing to acknowledge them.

Well, tough shit because there was nothing on this planet that could make him trust Dixie again, much less let her back into his life, even on a small scale. If she was here to win him back, then she was about to be sorely disappointed, running back to wherever she lived with her tail between her legs, the scent of shame clinging to her.

Besides, he had no interest in getting back together with her anyway.

The last he heard of her she'd moved somewhere fancy and gotten a job at one of those soulless law firms, cash cows that were interested in making as much money off of people as possible, staring at them with nothing more than dollar signs in their eyes.

Basically, she'd sold out, traded her soul for a fancy penthouse, and a car that cost a ridiculous sum of money. Or, so he'd heard. Aiden hadn't been trying to keep tabs or anything; it was simply that they shared the same group of friends, so for the longest time, she was everywhere, in most conversations.

It wasn't as if he could ask them to stop talking about her altogether, ceasing to exist for that brief moment of time. To their credit, their friends had tried in the beginning, trailing off awkwardly whenever her name was brought up, and they shot him sympathetic looks, doing their best to steer the conversation away from her altogether, the red line clear.

Still, over time, they fell back into old patterns, and Dixie's name came up every now and again in passing, a beacon of hope and success for all of them. Aiden was the only who seemed disappointed, wanting nothing more than to tell Dixie that she was a sell-out.

Sure, she was comfortable enough now, but it didn't change the reality of things.

He waited for her to respond, to take up the mantel of self-righteous indignation and defend herself, but she stayed quiet, allowing him a wide berth of space to vent, years of building up what to say tumbling out, a torrent of suppressed emotion.

He had to admit, it felt better than he anticipated, but now that he no longer had the anger to hold onto, the barbed wire words that were supposed to bring her to her knees, inflicting the same amount of agonizing pain that she did on him; the hole in his heart was strangely empty.

"What do you want me to do, Aiden?" Dixie asked, dragging her gaze up to meet his, her dark eyes wide and unflinching, the apology swimming in the depths of her irises. "Do you want me to leave?"

"As a matter of a fact, I do," Aiden pointed out. "Is that what you wanted to ask me? If there's any reason for you to stay?"

A small kernel of hope blossomed inside his heart in spite of his best attempts to squash it, and he allowed himself a small reprieve, his eyes running over her, nostalgia dancing in his field of vision.

"No, actually. I meant what I said, Aiden. I don't want to relive the past. I hate the way things ended, but I can't change that, and I know I fucked up, but I can't change that either."

Aiden paused. "So, why did you come talk to me then?"

"I came to talk to you about Frankie," Dixie elaborated, hiking her purse up her shoulder.

"Who?"

"Franklin Deceasare," Dixie added, watching his face carefully. "My client."

His mind went blank, racing to fill in the blanks.

Of course.

Now, he felt like the world's biggest fool. There he was, pouring his heart out, allowing all the hurt and pain to manifest, looking for the closure he never got, when in reality, Dixie had simply cover to talk shop.

For a second, he'd forgotten that she was a lawyer too, had allowed that little tidbit of information to be pushed to the back of his mind, gathering dust in its irrelevancy.

Suddenly, he was embarrassed, having jumped the gun and assumed she couldn't possibly have anything else to talk about except for their history. As it turned out, there was a plethora of other subjects they could discuss, none of them relating to their personal lives.

Way to go, you dumb fuck. That wasn't professional at all, and now she's going to think you're unhinged or something. Worse, now she'll probably figure out a way to take you down in court.

Aiden squared his shoulders and uncrossed his arms, allowing them to fall limply at his side. "What about Franklin?"

"Look, I can't change the history between us, but you know Franklin didn't do it. The evidence against him is circumstantial at best."

"Really? Is that why you're sweating?"

Dixie sighed. "I'm not. I just think you're unfairly prosecuting my client, and I was hoping we could reach some kind of deal outside of court."

"You've got to be shitting me," Aiden muttered. "Why would I want to do that?"

"Because Franklin is innocent," Dixie emphasized. "And I know you've been coming at him hard, so I wanted to talk about that."

"You want to talk about it?"

Aiden scoffed. "Make a goddamn appointment, Dixie. Beyond that, I don't really give a shit what you have to say."

Chapter 3
Dixie

In all fairness, she deserved to be chewed out and spat back up for what she'd done to Aiden. Granted, he needn't have been so harsh, especially not when she beat herself up about it enough over the years, so many times that eventually she had to stop trying to run herself into the ground.

At the end of the day, she made the best decision she could at the time with what little experience she had.

Was it the best decision to make?

Honestly, she had no idea, but she did know that she didn't regret it, not one bit. Yes, it ended up eating away at the only real relationship she ever had, destroying it with one fatal blow, but she got to pursue her law career.

And for that she wouldn't apologize.

It wasn't as if she left Aiden for another man. Now, that would've been truly unforgivable, something she couldn't come back from, no matter how nicely she dressed it up, or how much she begged.

No, that was the sort of thing she herself couldn't forgive, and thus she expected nothing less from the people in her life especially in terms of romantic relationships. Aiden was no exception to that rule.

But he acted like her decision to uproot her life had been easy for her, a walk in the park compared to the pain he felt at being left behind. In reality, there were one too many times where she'd gotten into her car and drove halfway to San Francisco before she forced herself to turn back around, tears streaming down her face, and the pain in her chest radiating with unparalleled force.

Leaving Aiden had been fucking hard, and she didn't need him to keep reminding her of that, not every minute of the day. Because she already knew how difficult it was, and she suspected he thought she led a better life, shinier.

Sure, she had a nice cushy job, with a hell of a salary, but she made no apologies for the decisions she made, even if some people did believe she worked for the devil himself.

That couldn't be further from the truth.

Dixie may have wanted a comfortable life for herself, but she hadn't sacrificed her morals to get there, contrary to what many people believed. In fact, she was one of the few lawyers who fought tooth and nail to hold onto her integrity, the one thing she had left after leaving behind the only life she'd ever known, and the only man she would ever love.

If there was one thing Dixie refused to be called, it was a leech, a parasite who lived off of others, sucking their blood to survive and generally mooching off of other species.

She knew full well that was the way most people viewed lawyers, nothing but a shiny suit and fancy briefcase, meant to take as much money as they could before they hit the road, leaving skid marks behind.

Dixie was proud to say that she was not like that, at all.

Impatient, she tapped her feet against the steps and checked her watch, cursing under her breath as she noticed how late Aiden actually was. After their confrontation at the pub, she expected a bit more resistance in terms of interacting with her, but he seemed to accept that, whether he liked it or not, they were going to be dealing with each other face to face.

It was better for all parties involved if they put their issues behind them and focused on the present, like the mature and responsible adults they were. Dixie sighed and ran her fingers through her hair, lifting it up off the nape of her neck to allow a cool breeze to tickle the back of her neck.

Truthfully, she had no idea if this was normal behavior in Aiden's book, tardiness, but she wanted to give him the benefit of the doubt, so she spread out a folded old newspaper and sat gingery, drawing her knees to her chest, and her eyes fixed on the road ahead, offering her an ample view of the cars coming and going.

Also, the people.

Finally, she spotted a familiar head of hair, rounding the corner at an unhurried pace, dressed impeccably in a dark gray suit that brought out the hues of gray in his piercing blue eyes.

With his briefcase at his side, and his other hand shoved in his pocket, he made her heart squeeze painfully, a hollow reminder of what she walked out on, and she stood up, brushing off imaginary lint and tossing her hair behind her shoulder.

Based on their current record, she doubted this meeting would go any better, but she had to at least try, for the sake of her client, and her brother who owed her a hell of a lot more than an all you can eat sushi meal and full steak dinner.

All at once, she was struck with the sudden urge to up her price, given how difficult Aiden was being. His eyes landed on her, and he raised an eyebrow, but didn't give any other reaction.

She stepped in front of him and plastered a professional smile onto her features. "Mr. Lawson. I think we should talk about my client. Is now a good time?"

He barely spared her a glance as he walked past. "Make an appointment."

Just like that, he brushed past her, and she froze, staring after him with her mouth agape. Here she was, trying to be bigger the person by meeting him, and he just walked past like her she was some novice, a freaking second year law student.

Furious, she snatched her briefcase and stomped inside, requesting a meeting with Mr. Lawson through gritted teeth, feeling the urge to throw something across the room, hard.

By all accounts, it seemed Aiden was never going to forgive her for leaving him to go to school in Georgetown instead of attending Stanford Law, and she wasn't entirely sure she could blame him.

From his perspective, he was justified, and from hers, she was.

Round and round they went on the merry go round, with no sign of slowing down.

She inhaled in through her nose and out through her mouth, noisily breathing as she set up an appointment with Mr. Lawson. Minutes later, she was shown into a conference room inside the nondescript building, and she paced to the other end of the room, needing to be as much space between them as possible.

It appeared that, much like five years ago, they were still able to get under each other's skin, but it was worse than before because she had no way of making it better, of putting out the fire in her heart.

All too soon, far before she was ready, Aiden stepped in, his tie askew, and his suit jacket draped across his arm. In an unhurried manner, he set it out across the chair and shut the door behind him with a soft click, leaving them alone with nothing but a big mahogany table, and the heater in the background.

"You wanted to see me?" Aiden asked, crossing one ankle over the other and gesturing for her to speak.

Arrogant asshole.

"Yes, I did. We still haven't discussed my client."

"So, I guess things have changed since you and I were together because the Dixie I knew never would've agreed to represent a murderer."

Dixie frowned. "Franklin is not a murderer, and I would appreciate if it you would refrain from calling him that. Innocent until proven guilty, remember?"

Aiden scoffed. "The evidence speaks for itself, Ms. Aricello, and his name is written all over this particular crime scene."

"You are missing the motive," Dixie pointed out, smugly.

Aiden's expression faltered before he brushed her comment away. "I'm sure something will turn up before the trial."

"What makes you so sure?" Dixie demanded.

"Because I know for a fact he's guilty and getting himself a fancy ass lawyer isn't going to change that," Aiden replied, voice dripping with acid. "I don't care how things are done in Georgetown, but over here, we talk the law seriously, and we don't do anyone any favors. It seemed your law school degree isn't as useful as you thought."

Bastard.

"How dare you?" Dixie demanded. "You know as well as I that I am a damn good lawyer, and that Georgetown is one of the best law schools around. You just can't stand to admit it. As for your not so subtle insinuation, Franklin is my brother's friend, and he asked if I could take the case. There's no rule against that."

"Unless it colors your judgment," Aiden grumbled, darkly.

"You mean like your bias is clouding yours?" Dixie challenged, placing her hands on either side of the desk. "You're letting your own personal feelings get in the way of doing your job."

"At least I'm capable of feeling something," Aiden spat out. "Unlike you. Tell me, Dixie. Was it worth it? Was Georgetown worth throwing away everything we had?"

"For fuck's sake, Aiden. You know that I had little choice in the matter. Georgetown was my dream, and you knew that."

"You could've gone to Stanford law," Aiden pointed out, churlishly. "But instead you chose to leave everything behind, including me just to pursue a degree in a college that could never appreciate you, not even if it tried."

"That's not true," Dixie protested. "I worked my ass off there, and I graduated at the top of my class, for your information."

"So, was it worth it?" Aiden repeated, circling around the desk, his expression taunting. "Dumping me for your degree?"

His words stung, like being slapped across the face, the angry red welt pulsing and obvious.

"It wasn't like that. You know it wasn't," Dixie argued. "I had to go because this was my future, and you were asking me to give it up, which wasn't fair."

"So, you chose a mediocre law degree over me?" Aiden asked.

"It wasn't like that for me, Aiden, and you know it. I was young back then, and I wanted to go after my dream. Besides, I told you that we could do the long distance thing, and you're the one who said no, or have you forgotten that?"

Aiden snorted. "Of course I said no to that. Long distance is hard, and it does nothing but chip away at the relationship little by little till there is nothing left."

Like ripping off a band aid slowly, pausing every so often instead of yanking it off all at once.

"I couldn't allow that to happen to us," Aiden continued, eyes blazing. "So I did what I had to do, but you didn't have to abandon me."

Dixie exhaled. "Look, Aiden you have to believe me when I say this. If there was any other way, I would've taken it, but I thought there couldn't possibly be, and it killed me to have to make that choice, but I made it because I thought it was the right thing to do."

Aiden's mouth slammed shut, but he said nothing, drawing to a halt a few feet away, watching her carefully.

"But there is not a day that goes by that I don't miss you, that I don't wonder what would've happened if I'd taken the risk in Stanford," Dixie added, her voice immeasurably small.

She swallowed past the lump in her throat, hardly able to believe she was being this forward with him when she swore she'd take it to her grave. However, he deserved the truth, whatever that was worth.

It wouldn't provide much in the way of solace, and it couldn't give them a clean slate, but it would ease some of the bitterness.

"I know I screwed up, Aiden, but I can't change what I did even though I am sorry for it."

Before she knew what was happening, Aiden had crossed the room in two strides, tilted her chin up and pressed his lips to hers, the world around her shifting and tilting before it faded away, receding into background noise.

Just like that, her knees buckled.

Chapter 4
Aiden

Aiden could tell the exact moment her hesitance melted away, and that was when she no longer held still against his mouth, instead wrapping her arms around his neck and deepening the kiss.

In the back of her mouth, she made a soft whimpering noise, and it made Aiden's body react as a response, pressing himself closer, his hands falling to the small of her waist.

Of their own accord, his hands began moving all over body, starting from her ears, down to the curve of her hips, caressing every inch of available skin, charting a familiar path he'd wandered a million times before.

Damn.

She felt just as good as she remembered, and the fire between them was obviously just as real and alive now as it was back then. In fact, Aiden hadn't even been sure what he'd been doing until he crossed the room and took her into his arms, unable to bear it any longer.

This.

This felt more than good, it felt right.

Her hands fell from his shoulders down to his ass, and she ran her fingers over it, making soft little mewling noises in the process. Then, she went around and cupped him over the fabric of his trousers, pressing slightly.

Aiden growled, all the blood going straight to his groin, a thick fog of desire settling over him, so he couldn't think straight. All he could see or hear or taste was Dixie, and he wouldn't have it any other way.

His hands dropped down to her legs, and he hoisted her up, maneuvering them backwards until she hit the back of the table, and he set her down, kicking her legs apart, so he could settle there, pressing against her center.

She ran her hands over his back, snaking under his shirt, her soft touch making goosebumps ripple across his entire body, a visceral response that surprised him. Slowly, she brought her hands back around to the front and began to undo the buttons till she pushed his shirt backwards, wrapping her legs firmly around his waist.

Before long, she was raking her hands across his back, panting as he pulled away and started peppering her neck with kisses, fumbling with the buttons on her shirt, eager to get it off.

Soon, he grew impatient and tugged, the sound of fabric ripping echoing back to them in the empty room as his mouth moved down, his hands moving around to unhook her bra from the back.

Her breasts sprung forward, and he lowered his gaze, his tongue darting out to lick each nipple before he tugged hard, enjoying the look of pure delight on her face. With her hair wrapped in a high ponytail, with a few wisps escaping, her head thrown back, and her eyes screwed shut, she looked like the picture of wild and reckless abandonment.

A small thrill raced up his spine at the thought that he was the one responsible for this, she was experiencing ecstasy at his hands, not anyone else's. That thought swirled around his brain as his hands skirted over her skin, down her navel, all the way to her waist line.

Next, the pants were zipped down, and he took his sweet time, even as Dixie made soft little whimpers of protest, kicking her legs around in an attempt to make him move faster. He placed one hand on her thigh to hold her still while the other slid the pants off, tossing them into a heap in the corner.

His lips sought out hers once more, claiming and demanding, his tongue darting out to lick lightly. She gasped and parted her mouth, her tongue connecting with his, a sensual battle for dominance.

Her bare breasts pressed against his skin, the nipples hard as pebbles, making his erection grow harder till it was straining through the fabric of his boxers, demanding to be let out.

As if she sensed his train of thought, her hand dropped between them, and she yanked off his pants, letting them pool around his ankles, her hands quickly ducking underneath the boxers and touching the tip.

It jumped in response, and she smiled into the kiss, pushing down the boxers, so they joined his pants, wrapped around the bottom of his legs. He pressed himself into her hand, wanting her to keep touching him, and to keep pushing him over the edge.

He dropped his head to the crook of her shoulder and sucked in a harsh breath as she ran her fingers all over him, feather light and teasing, using only the tip of her index finger, and her thumb.

Fuck.

He had no idea that something as simple as a light touch could drive him this wild. It was taking every ounce of self-control he had to hold himself still, to stop himself from just prying her thighs open and thrusting into her.

Obviously, he wanted her to enjoy herself, and she seemed to be enjoying this part, reacquainting herself with the parts of him she'd allowed to rust, to be pushed to the back of her mind in order to survive.

Dixie remained unusually quiet as she ran her fingers over him, up and down then sideways, setting a path before she traced his happy trail back up to his neck, tugging slightly on his earlobes.

He groaned, and drew his mouth back, sinking his teeth into her neck. She hissed, and her grip slackened, tilting her neck to the side to offer him better access. He sucked, wanting to leave a mark for her to remember him by before he gently pulled away and kissed it, drawing back to look at her face.

Her eyes were full of hunger and need, melting pools of chocolate. He leaned forward and captured her lips with his, her hands falling to her side as she gripped his shoulders. With precision, he guided himself into her, stilling as he waited for her to adapt, expanding.

A soft sigh fell from her lips as she pressed herself closer, flexing her thighs. She dropped a kiss to his shoulder before she leaned in and started panting into his ear, recalling how the noises she used to make tempted him, making the blood in his body feel like molten lava.

On cue, his body responded, and he rotated his hips, easing into the movement as she tossed her head back and bit down on her lips hard, barely holding back the moan that threatened to give them away.

Her hands dropped to his ass, and her nails dug in, leaving small marks everywhere touched, her own brand of territorial as he started to pick up the pace, easing out of her before he thrust back in.

Dixie sat on the table, with her legs on either side of her, completely still, letting him do all the work, as if she was afraid to respond, terrified of what might happen if she met each thrust with one of her own.

Aiden pushed himself into her, marveling at the gasp of surprise before her hips started to circle, setting up a rhythm of their own. He smirked and thrust deeper, licking a path from her navel all the way up to her ears where he paused and started whispering.

The dirtier his words got, the more she seemed to respond, her movements increasing till they became frenzied, devoid of any kind of second guessing or insecurity.

In that moment, Dixie let herself go, and Aiden was enjoying every minute of it, varying his speed and technique, driving her closer and closer to the edge as she squirmed underneath him, panting and writhing with pleasure.

A small voice in the back of his mind wondered if this was a good idea, if they weren't just falling back into old habits all over again, but he viciously shoved it away, choosing instead to focus on the way she felt wrapped around him, and how warm she was.

Oh, how he'd missed her.

No one in the world was able to drive him crazy the way she did, or make him feel as if he was starving for affection, his appetite insatiable unless he was deep within her, pushing her over the edge repeatedly.

Her body trembled beneath him, and he increased the thrusts, the blood singing in his ears as she climaxed, spasming wildly, her mouth parted slightly as a thin sheen of sweat broke out across her forehead.

Aiden waited for her to come off her high before he pressed a soft kiss to her lips and spun her around. He placed her hands on either side of the desk, making sure she had a tight grip before he lifted her ass up and slid in, grunting as she let out a yelp of approval, one hand reaching behind her to thread her fingers through his hair, tugging painfully.

His head fell forward, resting on her shoulders as he growled, driving himself into her over and over, trying to erase everything that had happened between them, replacing it with nothing but good memories and nights spent worshipping each other's bodies.

This was how it was supposed to be.

The two of them intertwined around each other, the sound of skin slapping against skin, sweat pouring down their backs steadily. Once again, Dixie flew over the edge, his name a soft chant she hummed under her breath, the sound of her uneven breathing filling the room.

Slowly, she hoisted herself up and spun around, placing her hands on his chest before she captured her lips with his, searing and all encompassing. He wrapped his arms around her waist before his hands found their way up to her hair, tangling themselves in her thick locks.

Dixie moaned and pushed him back, so the back of his legs hit the table. Before he knew what was happening, he was on his back, and she was climbing on top of him, her tits bouncing up and down as she rode him, hard.

As if they had a mind of his own, his hands came up to her hips and dug in, controlling her movement as he bit down on his bottom lip and watched her, the way she reveled in the control she had over him.

Holy fucking shit.

He'd never seen anything more beautiful in his entire life, and he wanted to stay like that for hours, days even, doing nothing but feeling himself deep inside of her, their own little bubble heedless of the outside world.

Unable to bear it any longer, he growled and pushed his head back, taking one breast into his mouth, his tongue circling around the sensitive nub while his hand kneaded the other, teasing, tempting until they were both as hard as rocks, and Dixie was making unintelligible noises under her breath, her hands gripping either side of the table.

Eventually, her body writhed, prompting his own release, and she collapsed against him, slick with sweat, her head finding the familiar spot in the crook of his neck. His arms came up around her, on automatic, pressing her to him as he sniffed her hair, allowing the smell of her to engulf him.

Gradually, her breath evened out, and as it did, she stiffened, her body taut as she stirred and pushed herself up, refusing to meet his gaze. Faster than he would've imagined, she slid herself off of him and adjusted her hair, her eyes dancing around the room.

Without uttering a single word, she picked up her pants and wriggled into them, zipping them back up. Then, she reached for her jacket, shaking her head at the torn piece of fabric that used to be her blouse.

She tucked it into her jacket pocket and adjusted her blazer, so it would look as if nothing was amiss. Aiden watched her, his head resting on his elbow, waiting for her to say something.

In a second, she was gone, the door slamming shut behind her.

Chapter 5
Dixie

No.

No.

No.

She had no idea what possessed her to sleep with Aiden, of all people. Granted, they had a connection, and a long and complicated history, particularly because of how it ended, but she firmly believed it was the absolute worst possible thing she could've done.

Basically, she hadn't done herself any favors by giving into the desire, bubbling beneath the surface. Especially because things weren't the same now; they were different people, no longer the idealistic youth who'd met during senior year of college and moved in together a year later.

No, she wasn't that person anymore, not even close.

Being out in the real world had changed her, and she liked to think it made her better, smart. At the very least, it gave her thicker skin, something she was sorely lacking, but now, she felt like that insecure young adult again.

Curse the luck that made her have to choose between the love of her life and the school of her dreams. It was strange how one encounter with Aiden brought it all back: the heartache, the indecision, and the insecurity at the root of it all.

Honestly, she wasn't even sure how it had happened.

One minute, they were screaming at each other across the room, fleshing out the bitter couple who'd ended things on bad terms, and the next they were all over each other, barely able to get enough of each other.

What the hell?

She didn't like how off kilter Aiden made her feel. For years after she left, she worked hard to make sure she stayed on her feet, that she exercised control over every aspect of her life, never wanting herself to be that vulnerable young woman again, blubbering over a man.

And for a while there, she thought she had it down to a science, having perfected the method, but all it took was one kiss from Aiden, and snap, just like that, all her walls were shattered, silently, and she'd stepped over the debris, throwing her rule back right out the window.

There was a reason it was a bad idea to get involved with exes.

At the end of the day, no matter how great it was, there was a reason they were in your past not your present, and she had to actively remind herself of that. Sure, Aiden was her match in all the ways that counted, and it was the only relationship in her life where she was secure and happy.

But, it didn't change the fact.

When it came right down to it, it got bad, uglier than she'd anticipated, and she couldn't change that, or wipe it away from her memory with an eraser, leaving nothing but smudges and a faint recollection of what used to be there.

Her body on the other hand had, clearly, not gotten the memo. Half of her had turned into mush when he touched her, panting and begging for more, needing to feel as much of him as possible, before the voice of reason managed to break through, wagging its finger at her recklessness.

Unfortunately, she'd managed to subdue her conscience long enough to get busy with Aiden, and it wasn't until they were done, and she was laying there, pressed up against him that it dawned on her.

Slamming into her with the force of a tidal wave.

Sleeping with Aiden had been a mistake, not just because of their history but also because of the fact that they worked together. In fact, she had no idea how to face him now that they'd seen each other like that, experienced each other in that way.

Fuck.

She raked her fingers through her hair then ran her hands over her face, trying to focus on the words in front of her. Frustrated, she pushed back against the chair, hearing it scrape against the floor as she stood up and bent down to touch her toes.

Slowly, she lifted her arms up and bent her knees, repeating the gesture a few times to clear her head, counting silently under her breath until some of the tension seeped away from her body.

If only it were that easy to get rid of Aiden and all thoughts pertaining to him. As it was, she was acting like a petulant child around him, going out of her way to avoid him whenever she saw him coming down the hallway, and instructing her team to take a message whenever he called.

A part of her was horrified at the immature behavior, but she needed time to regroup, and to get her hormones back in order before she would have no choice but to face him.

Besides, she couldn't avoid him forever, not with the trial coming up, and she'd never been more thankful for a case like this, something she could sink her teeth into and dive in headfirst.

Focusing on her client, and his needs, kept her from dwelling on hers even if she had made little in the way of progress, frustratingly. In terms of evidence, Franklin was completely screwed, and she understood why Aiden and his team already felt like it was a slam-dunk.

In all honesty, the evidence wasn't helping her case at all, even if some of it was circumstantial, and although her faith in Frankie's innocence hadn't wavered, she was starting to doubt her ability to get the trial dismissed.

Obviously, she didn't like feeling uncertain.

More than anything in the world, she wanted to find that hidden inconsistency, comb through the files until she found the one that shed enough doubt, so she could blow the whole thing wide open.

Luckily, she had nothing but time on her hands, and a primary suspect already in mind. By all accounts, she was ready to walk away from the case, especially when she found out that Franklin was mixed up with the crime life.

In fact, she'd all but walked out there until she saw how contrite Franklin was, the fear evident in his eyes. In that moment, she'd been certain that if she won the case for him, he would turn over a new leaf, forsaking the life of crime he'd waded into.

However, the same issue remained, as persistent as a weed. Franklin hadn't committed the crime, that much was obvious to her, but if he hadn't then it meant that someone higher up on the food chain had.

A high level mob boss or something.

And that led her to the same conclusion, highlighted in a big bold red pen in her notes: Israel Regatta. Notorious crime lord, and some even said he was on the same level as Pablo Escobar though she had her doubts.

Regatta was nothing like the infamous Cuban drug dealer, not even close, but he had made a name for himself, and based on all the intel she could find, he'd spent his entire life building up to it.

According to the research, Regatta had been in and out of juvie since he was old enough to be sentenced, and before that, he was described by many as the troublemaker on the block.

Now, being mischievous at a young age hadn't been enough to set off any warning flags. On the contrary, many eyewitness reports stated that they believed he was a good man underneath it all, but obviously somewhere along the line, he'd stopped splitting hairs and just went all in.

Investing completely until he became a different person.

Her digging had led her to the local authorities who'd informed her, with grim expression that they'd been on his case for years, carefully cataloguing anything out of place, and patiently waiting for the day when he'd slip up.

Everyone did inevitably and Regatta was no exception.

All they had to do was bide their time till the right piece of evidence gave them all the jurisdiction they needed to put him away. Unfortunately, that was a much bigger case, one she wasn't currently working.

Yes, Regatta was bad news, but at the moment, he wasn't her problem, and she'd prefer to sweep him under the rug and focus on her client. Israel had to be his boss, and for some reason, in his book, it was far easier to frame a lower level gangster than to make sure the breadcrumbs led somewhere else.

It had to be the explanation. Otherwise, she had diddly squat.

For a man who'd been doing it for years, he had the seasoned expertise and calm of a professional, someone comfortable in his own skin, who knew exactly what his place was in the world and happily took up the mantel.

Dixie had no interest in getting caught in the crosshairs, collateral damage in whatever turf war was happening. Of course she wasn't certain that was the case here, but she couldn't come up with any other reason why Regatta would risk exposing himself with a rookie mistake.

A murder was no small thing, and it was sure to attract attention, and not the good kind, so it made sense that the crime boss would want the trail to run cold, to lead them far away from him, and his sweet set up.

So, it didn't add up.

Why would Regatta go through all that trouble, taking precautions and making a plethora of contingency plans, just to be safe only to turn around and point the finger at one of his own?

Granted, Franklin didn't work for Regatta, not directly, but they were in the same business, and they had this shared notion that brothers in arms stood united, fighting against capture and someone pulling the curtains back to reveal their true selves.

Frustrated, Dixie tossed her pen on the table, watching it bounce around before it landed with a thump onto the floor, rolling away somewhere she wouldn't be able to find. She sighed and stood up, walking from end of the room the other.

Weeks.

That was how long she'd been at this, working to crack what was shaping up to be one of the most difficult cases of her life, and she wasn't even sure if she had even more energy to give.

Running on fumes wasn't easy, and if she coupled that with her active efforts to stay as far away from Aiden as she possibly could without compromising her professional integrity, had proven to be challenging.

But she wasn't ready to face him regardless.

Really, it should be much simpler than she was making it out to be. All she had to do was keep her professional smile in place, shake his hand and have it out in a courtroom, praying he didn't say anything even remotely antagonizing, so she wouldn't lose it right then and there.

In theory, it sounded easy enough, but in reality, it was anything about. Aiden was a wild card, the kind she couldn't predict or see coming, and she had no idea what he was going to try to do next.

God help her.

She twisted her neck all the way to the right before she repeated the step on the other side, twisting her arms behind her shoulders. Her body was lethargic, moving as if it were powered by a low energy system, affecting her central nervous system.

Don't think about Aiden. Think about Franklin who needs you. His entire life is on the line here, and you need to make sure he gets out of it, no matter what you do.

With that thought firmly in mind, she pored over the case once more, jotting down notes and allowing coffee and salads to help her power through, breaking the routine every so often with a cookie.

This was not the first time Israel had pinned a case on a lower level gangster, nor would it be the last, but the least Dixie could do was try to help at least one victim. The rest would follow.

Finally, she was ready to face him.

Chapter 6
Aiden

He liked to think of himself as a man who wasn't easily affected, who managed to keep his cool while everyone around him lost their nerve, and so far that had been the case, with his steel iron will serving him well.

Hell, he'd spent enough time perfecting that attitude and was glad it was finally paying off. At least until Dixie walked back into his life and screwed everything up. Granted, it was normal for an ex to shake things up when they came back, but not like this.

Seeing her standing a few feet away from him, head bent low in conversation, reminded him of their little escapade in the conference room. In a flash, it all came back to him, and he gritted his teeth in response especially as he tried to push the memory away and focus on the fact that she left him.

Again.

Really, he shouldn't have been surprised, but he had been. Like a fool, he'd sat there, a part of him truly believing she would come back, but when the minutes ticked by and nothing changed, he'd leapt up and got dressed, berating himself for making the first move to begin with.

And for what?

Because he wanted to fuck her?

Admittedly, it was the best sex he'd had in years, and he wasn't above acknowledging that, but it wasn't worth the hassle that came along with it, not even close.

In the weeks that followed, he'd tried to get a hold of her, convincing himself that it was strictly for business purposes given looming date of their case, but he'd always missed her by a hair.

After a while, it became clear that she was avoiding him, preferring to act as if the whole thing had never happened, and they could just face each other without it being an issue.

Well, two could play at that game.

No sooner had the thought left his mind than Dixie turned around, and his mouth went dry, his body twitching in reaction to the tight business suit she was wearing, hugging her body in all the right places with her stopping just above her breasts, emphasized in her shirt.

Shit.

Get a grip, Aiden. You're not a hormonal high schooler. You're a grown ass man.

The suit looked eerily similar to the one she wore the day they stood on opposite sides of the conference room, screaming at each other before they ended up tearing each other's clothes off, barely able to get enough, but it didn't matter.

Facts were facts, and although Dixie clearly still affected him on some level, subconsciously at least, invoking his basic desire, she was still no good for him, her betrayal ringing out clearly in his head.

He couldn't allow himself to forget the fact that she left him to pursue her law career. Privately, he could acknowledge that he was proud of her for sticking it out, for achieving her dreams and more, but it didn't mean it hurt any less.

The bitter sting of betrayal still lingered, and if her reaction in the conference room was any indication then she hadn't changed a bit, preferring to put her own needs above anyone else's.

With that thought firmly lodged in his mind, his reaction to her lessened, and he was able to push the lust away firmly, allowing the door to slam shut and throwing away the key.

Honestly, it was better this way especially considering they were both about to go in for the first day of trial, and she didn't stand a chance. He felt a miniscule amount of pity for her, recognizing that she was about to have her ass handed back to her on a silver platter, but it was her own fault for taking on this case pro bono.

She had no business doing that anyway, and he couldn't for the life of him figure out why, but it wasn't any of his business. All he needed was to step through the door, and the rest would play out like a choreographed dance.

He shoved his hands in his pockets and checked his watch, noting that there were only a few minutes left till they were up. Confidently, he ran his fingers over his suit and straightened his back, repeating the same upbeat mantra inside his head.

Finally, it was their turn, and Dixie brushed past him, the smell of her perfume lingering behind her. He stiffened, willing himself not to sniff it, but against his better judgment he did, and he was perplexed, taking stock of the smug look on Dixie's face.

Something was up.

In his efforts to keep some distance between them, he'd failed to notice that she looked like she was about to break out into a dance, barely containing her excitement. In fact, she wasn't even bothering to hide it, leaning over to whisper in Franklin's ear, his smile stretching from one corner to another.

Aiden narrowed his eyes and leaned forward in his chair, as if it would help him figure out what was happening. Clearly, she had some kind of ace up her sleeve, or she wouldn't be leaning back languidly, looking like she could be on a beach somewhere sipping a mojito.

All at once, they all stood up, waiting for the judge to walk in, and she did, quickly taking a familiar seat before she gestured for them all to sit once more. As soon as she announced the case, Dixie wasted no time in asking for an acquittal.

"I beg your pardon, Ms. Aricello?" Judge Loretta asked, clasping her hands together and frowning. "You are aware that the notion was denied before based on insufficient grounds."

"Yes, your honor, I am aware of that," Dixie acknowledged, undoing the first button on her jacket. "But I am also aware that the murder weapon in question was never found."

Judge Loretta slid her gaze over to Aiden who stood up and cleared his throat. "That's right, your honor. It wasn't, but I fail to see how that has any relevance on the matter at hand."

"Because the murder weapon was found," Dixie pointed out.

Fuck.

So this was why Dixie was acting like she was all that; it wasn't false bravado, or some kind of act to get herself psyched up. She literally held the most dangerous weapon in her hand, the ability to change the entire course of the game, and she wasn't holding back her punches.

"What?" Aiden asked, swallowing past the lump in his throat. "You couldn't have. A team of experts searched high and low for the murder weapon, and not a single trace of it was found."

Dixie shrugged. "I guess they didn't look hard enough because I was able to find it when I went back and examined the crime scene, hidden underneath a loose tile in the bathroom ceiling of all places."

Aiden's brows knitted together, and he glanced down at his notes, for once, at a complete loss regarding what to say or what to do. The authorities had insisted that the weapon was nowhere to be found, even went so far as to assure him Franklin would be sentenced without any kind of problems.

But that was before the murder weapon conveniently turned up at enemy base, wielded like some sort of, well, weapon. He stood up taller and shoved his hands in his pockets.

"Why wasn't this evidence brought to light sooner?" Aiden inquired, attempting to keep a professional veneer even as he watched the jury exchange looks, sympathy already sprouting up.

No, he couldn't lose the case, not like this.

Not when he was so close.

He was sure Franklin was guilty; he had to be.

"Because I was only able to find it last night," Dixie responded, reaching behind the desk for a sealed plastic bag. "Don't worry. I had gloves on when I was searching."

Judge Loretta leaned back in her chair, a pained expression crossing her features as she motioned them forward. "Please approach the bench."

Together, they approached, keeping as much space between them as possible, gazing up at the weathered face of a woman who looked like she would rather be anywhere else.

"In light of new evidence, I will give you one hour, Mr. Lawson to perform the necessary tests and see if what Ms. Aricello is saying is true."

"An hour?" Aiden sputtered, mind racing. "Your Honor, that's barely enough time."

"Will it or will it not work?" Judge Loretta inquired, pinning him with an annoyed look. "I need an answer, Mr. Lawson, or the whole case will be postponed for another week."

Aiden nodded, begrudgingly. "I'll tell them to step on it, your honor."

"That's more like it," Judge Loretta pointed out, giving him an approving look before she turned to Dixie whose lips twitched, the desire to gloat hovering beneath the surface. "Ms. Aricello, I'd like to congratulate you on your detective work, but I'd suggest you leave that up to the professionals since it isn't your job."

Dixie's expression dimmed, and her smile faltered. "Yes, your honor."

"Court will reconvene in an hour. Dismissed."

She picked up the gravel and struck it against the sound block, its vibrations echoing back to them, much louder than he expected. He tossed Dixie a look over his shoulder, but she was already back at the table, conversing with Franklin who looked relieved.

Aiden knew the tests were just a formality because Dixie wouldn't risk throwing away her entire career falsifying evidence just to prove a point. No, she wouldn't hinge her career on it, so she'd done her research and knew exactly what she was doing.

Everything else was just a formality.

Still, he had to at least go through the motions, churn up the paperwork, so it could be over and done with. With the weapon tucked under his arm, he hurried off, off to seek answers he already knew.

But there was a small niggling voice in the back of his mind that persisted, convinced that she couldn't possibly have found it on her own. Yet, if Franklin were the one who handed it to her then he risked going away anyway, for tampering with evidence even if he was innocent.

****

"Your honor, Ms. Aricello was right," Aiden admitted, holding up the murder weapon in his right hand, slowly turning it around the room. The words tasted like acid going down his throat, and he hated it, but the truth was the truth, and she'd uncovered it fair and square.

"This weapon is what was used to kill the victim," Aiden concluded.

"Ladies and gentlemen of the jury, I would also like to point out that it is the primary weapon in six other murder cases," Dixie pointed out, the corners of her mouth turned down. This particular tidbit of news wasn't something she wanted to share, toeing the title of bearer of bad news. "That's actually how I was able to find it, your honor, by looking at evidence relating to other similar murders."

"Mr. Lawson?" Judge Loretta prompted, gesturing for him to respond.

Aiden bit back his irritation. "She's right, your honor."

"In that case, I have no choice but to dismiss all charges against Mr. Decesare on grounds of insufficient evidence. Mr. Descare, you are free to go. Case dismissed."

Dixie grinned as she patted Franklin on the back and was immediately surrounded by a crowd of well-wishers, soaking up the praise like a flower left in the sun.

Aiden sighed and spun around, shuffling through the many sheets of paper and taking his time organizing them, not wanting to face the media frenzy outside. Needless to say, his bosses wouldn't be pleased, but there was nothing he could've done.

Even if he had seen it coming, it didn't change the reality of the situation.

Begrudgingly, he had to accept defeat.

Dixie: 1.

Aiden: 0.

Chapter 7
Dixie

Yes.

After weeks of sleepless nights and running on fumes made of coffee and take-out food, she could finally congratulate herself on a job well done. As if that wasn't enough, wiping the smug smirk off of Aiden's face had only made her victory that much sweeter.

No, she wasn't a vindictive person, not in the slightest, but she had to admit that there was some small satisfaction to be gleaned from the fact that she managed to unearth the one piece of evidence that yanked the rug out from underneath Aiden's feet.

Turning the whole case on its heels and bringing the proceedings to a grinding halt.

Damn, it felt good, and she was going to enjoy every minute of that, knowing that she managed to beat Aiden even when he underestimated her, and the odds were against her.

Years later, when she carried around the weight of what she did to him, it was nice to look at him and not feel like she was being punched in the gut, repeatedly. Now, she could finally look at him and see him as nothing more than a colleague.

And the only man you've ever loved, her mind added quietly.

Dixie pushed away the voice in the back of her mind that told her to slow her horses and not break out the celebrate champagne just yet. Instead, she practically skipped out of the courthouse, blazer thrown over her shoulders, and a triumphant smile on her features.

Her hands flew up to her eyes to shield her from the afternoon soon, and she paused, enjoying the sweet high of victory, her eyes dancing across the street. Honestly, now that it was over, she had no idea what she wanted to do, but she did know that she didn't want to stand on the steps of the courthouse, in the heat.

In fact, she needed a cold drink.

With that thought in mind, she took out her phone, pulled up Google maps and looked up the nearest bar. Her eyes squinted in concentration as she put her hand atop her screen, trying to block out the sun as she scanned the list.

Finally, she settled on a place a few minutes' walk from where she was. Dixie straightened her back, adjusted the purse atop her shoulder and set off, her heels clicking loudly against the steps.

Sweat broke out across her forehead, and she frowned, using the back of her head to wipe it away. She glanced down at her phone, relieved to see that the bar in question was only a few feet away.

She glanced up, pushed the door open and sagged in relief when a blast of cold air came through. It was one of those rare days when the weather couldn't quite seem to make up its mind, and she was glad she'd decided to go for a heavy blazer and lighter clothes underneath otherwise she would've sweated right through them.

Instantly, she made a beeline for the bar and hopped onto the stool, flagging down a waiter and asking for a cold glass of water and a screwdriver. Dixie leaned back in her seat and fanned herself, her eyes scanning the place.

Unsurprisingly, there were few people around given the time of day, and those who were there were scattered around the wooden tables, heads bent over and nursing their drinks.

Overhead, there was a small TV set to the local news channel, the volume barely carrying over the sound of music wafting through the speakers. She twisted in her seat and studied the place, making note of the bathroom sign in the back, and the autographed pictures in the corner.

Back in the day, she imagined this must've been quite the hangout spot, with plenty of customers streaming in and out, and judging by the wall in the back, many famous ones at that.

Pity.

Now that the case was over, Dixie wasn't sure what her next move was. New York awaited her, her life and the career she had back there calling to her, a reminder of what she left behind, and she found her heart twist painfully in response.

Don't be stupid, Dixie. There's nothing for you here, anyway. You and Aiden are history.

She reached for her glass of water and took a long gulp, allowing the cool liquid to soothe her parched throat. Afterwards, she reached for her screwdriver and sipped, the liquid burning a path down her throat and settling in the pit of her belly, sending warmth to her extremities.

No, there was no need for her to dwell on it now. After all, she still had a few days left before she had to return, and she wanted to use that time to think about her next step, map out where she would go from here.

One thing was for sure; she couldn't stay in San Francisco.

There was nothing for her here, and there hadn't been in five years.

"Is this seat taken?"

She turned around and raised an eyebrow when she saw Aiden standing there in his suit, his tie hanging around his neck, and his sleeves rolled up to his forearms. More than that, he looked confused, as if she held all the answers he sought.

"No," Dixie replied, turning back to her drink.

She tensed when he hopped up next to her and ordered a beer, allowing them to lapse into silence, the weight of everything that had transpired hanging between them, a mountain.

"You did well there," Aiden commented, sounding impressed.

Dixie shrugged. "I was just doing my job."

"Well, I think it was great," Aiden reiterated.

"Even though I handed your ass to you?" Dixie asked, tossing him a long look.

Aiden shrugged. "Yeah, I guess so."

"Thanks," Dixie replied, uncertainty creeping into her tone. If he wasn't there to have a screaming match over the stunt she pulled, then why was he there? She couldn't figure out his motive.

"You're welcome," Aiden replied, without a trace of irony. He downed his drink in one gulp before he wiped his hand across his mouth and turned to face her, giving her his complete attention.

Feeling the weight of his gaze, she turned to look at him, resting her head in her hands. "What is it?"

"I want to ask you something," Aiden said, seriously.

"Okay."

"Why?" Aiden inquired, his blue eyes fathomless. She sighed and reached for her drink, needing a bit of liquid courage. Of course it was a rather loaded question, and she wasn't quite sure how to answer, if at all.

Why?

She wasn't even sure where to begin, but after all this time, she felt that Aiden deserved an answer, and it had nothing to do with their careers. Around her, the scenery blended into the background, becoming nothing more than white noise, a backdrop for this moment, one they'd been building towards for five years.

"Because of my dad," Dixie replied, the truth unfurling, the burden unfurling from around her heart. She watched his expression, ranging from disbelief to confusion before he gave a small shake of his head and gestured for her to continue.

"You know that my dad used to live in New York, right?" Dixie asked, tucking a lock of hair behind her ear.

Aiden nodded. "Yeah, I remember you telling me that, and I know you wanted to visit it, but why go to college there?"

Dixie took a deep breath, running her fingers over the outer rim of the glass, and trying to give her mind time to sort through the jumble of thoughts, ricocheting all over her brain, in no discernible order.

Truthfully, she didn't expect Aiden to understand, no did.

But at the end of the day, it didn't matter because she'd made her decision, and with the exception of her tainted memories of Aiden, hardened with the passage of time, she didn't regret it.

"My father had dreamed about going to Georgetown pretty much since he was a kid," Dixie began, swinging her legs back and forth, finding the motion oddly soothing. "Law school to be specific."

Aiden looked surprise, leaning backwards in his seat. "I didn't know that. You never told me."

Dixie shrugged. "It's not something I like to talk about. It was his dream to go here, not mine. He'd always wanted to end up back in New York, but it wasn't easy, you know. Life got in the way."

Admittedly, so had she.

Her parents had moved out to San Francisco, and she'd refused to leave whenever they mentioned New York, convinced that she couldn't possibly have a life away from the city by the bay, the only home she'd ever known.

Eventually, they stopped asking altogether, and Dixie realized, shamefully, that she was the one to blame. In fact, she held herself accountable for keeping her father from realizing his dream of going back.

"You have no idea what it felt for me to get the acceptance letter," Dixie whispered. Aiden leaned forward, straining to hear the rest of her story. "I felt like I could finally make him proud, you know."

Aiden frowned. "I'm sure he would've been proud of you anyway."

"Maybe, but I have no way of knowing," Dixie murmured, aware of their sudden proximity. As if she'd been electrocuted, she hastily withdrew, and turned towards her drink, using it as an excuse to turn away from him.

Dixie certainly hadn't expected this turn of events, the twist throwing her for a loop. All she wanted was to come to a bar and have a few drinks before she went back to the hotel for the night, spending the rest of her hours channel surfing till she fell asleep.

Now, much to her surprise, she was sitting across from the only man she'd ever loved, spilling her heart out to him, like she'd always dreamed of doing except she couldn't quite get a good read on him.

He looked puzzled, but at least he wasn't dismissive.

"Anyway, I wanted to make my father's dream come true," Dixie finished, signaling for another drink. "Even if it meant leaving my own happiness behind."

Aiden blinked and arched back, his hand going to his chin. "So, you went to Georgetown to honor your father?"

Dixie nodded. "I did, yeah. I know it sounds crazy, but I'd like to think that wherever he is, he's proud of me for making that dream come true. Somewhere along the line, Georgetown became my dream too, and I wanted to accomplish it for the both of us."

Aiden gulped. "I see."

"It had nothing to do with you," Dixie assured him, squeezing his hand and letting it linger for a few seconds before she placed it back in her lap. "I wanted to tell you, but I wasn't sure you'd understand."

"I think it's...noble," Aiden answered, after a momentary pause. "And I'm pretty sure your dad would be really proud."

"I hope so," Dixie said.

"Oh, he definitely would especially after you wiped the floor with my ass in court today," Aiden pointed out, traces of laughter in his tone. "If it were anyone else, I probably would've laughed and gotten myself kicked out."

Dixie smiled. "Is that so?"

Aiden smiled. "It is. As it is, I'm going to have a hell of a mess on my hands tomorrow. I have no idea how the hell you found that murder open, but they're going to chew me out for this."

"I'm sorry," Dixie offered.

"No, you aren't," Aiden pointed.

"You're right," Dixie agreed. "I'm not. Not entirely. I'm just sorry you're going to get an earful."

Aiden waved her comment away. "I think it's worth it. Do you want another drink?"

Dixie paused, war waging inside of her.

She was standing on the edge of a precipice, with the past calling out to her, and the future tugging her forward. Finally, she smiled and placed both arms on either side of the bar, drowning in his blue eyes.

"I'd love one."

Chapter 8
Aiden

Well, he felt like the world's biggest dick, and that was saying something.

Like most people in the world, he made a lot of questionable decisions in his life, but he tried not to regret them, firm in the belief that to do so would only cancel out the lessons he'd learned along the way.

However, there was one thing that stuck with him no matter what.

The way he and Dixie left things.

He remembered that day clearly in his mind's eye, so well in fact he could recite it from memory, every word, and every look. In fact, he could even recount what she'd been wearing that day, a knee length yellow dress that brought out the flecks of gold in her eyes.

More than that, he still couldn't shake off everything they'd said, the indecision that led to anger, giving way to some of the most hurtful things he'd ever uttered. Yes, Dixie had wanted to leave for Georgetown, and ultimately, it had created a wedge between them, but it wasn't the reason they broke up.

Not entirely.

At the end of the day, it was Aiden who'd refused to try, believing it was better to end then and there, on a high note before they dragged it through the mud even further. In his mind's eye, they'd already been heading downhill, and he hadn't seen the point in continuing.

Now, he definitely regretted it.

This entire time he'd lived secure in the knowledge that he'd made the right decision, choosing to put his own welfare first, protecting his own heart in favor of following her around like a lovesick puppy.

He couldn't have been more wrong.

There she'd been, attempting to make her father's dreams come true, by living it for him, and he'd done nothing but make her feel like shit for it, tossing out barbed wire words in an effort to hurt her for wanting to leave him.

And he had.

Actually, he hadn't even given her a chance to explain, cutting her off at every turn, convinced that she'd chosen Georgetown just to get away from him, to put as many miles between them as possible.

It hadn't occurred to him that her reasons for choosing Georgetown had nothing to do with him, not even close. Quite the contrary. Dixie was one of the most caring and selfless people she'd ever met, and he felt ashamed for not giving her the benefit of the doubt.

Half of him wanted to slam his head against a wall.

Repeatedly.

Instead, he reached for his drink and gulped it all, offering Dixie a sheepish grin. "Dix, I don't know what to say. I was a selfish bastard."

"Yes, you were," Dixie agreed. "But it was a really long time ago, Aiden, and you didn't know the truth."

"I should've known that there was a good reason," Aiden argued. "Instead of jumping to conclusions, I should've given you the benefit of the doubt."

The ghost of a smile flitted across Dixie's lips, one corner of her mouth tilting up. "Yeah, you should've, but you can't change the past."

No, he damn well couldn't.

But he could change the present.

Suddenly, all the anger and hurt he'd held onto, pressing it against his heart, and not allowing himself to forget, so he wouldn't get hurt again began to thaw, melting away little by little the more he thought about it.

Her story reached the farthest corners of his heart, and chipped away at the ice there, leaving nothing but warmth and nostalgia in its place, softening his entire stance.

Dixie wasn't the villain.

With that thought in mind, Aiden stood up and offered his hand, feeling clearer headed than he'd been in years. "Dance with me."

Dixie gave him a long look. "What? Since when do you dance?"

"Only with you," Aiden assured her.

She stared at him, war waging behind her irises before she stood up and slipped her hand into his, small and warm in his big, gruff ones. Slowly, he led her to the dance floor, drawing her close, so they were pressed against each other.

"I'm sorry, Dix," Aiden began. "I really am. I wish I'd known."

Dixie looked up at him, eyes softening. "I know, Aiden. Bygones, right?"

"I'd like that," Aiden replied, sincerity lacing his tone. "Only if you want to as well. Can you forgive me?"

"I want to," Dixie admitted.

"It's a start," Aiden pointed out, pressing his forehead to hers. Her hot breath danced across his face, and he allowed his eyes to flutter closed, inhaling the scent of her. "And I'll take what I can get at this point."

"Your dancing still hasn't improved," Dixie whispered, amused. "I thought you were going to take dance classes."

Aiden laughed. "I wanted to, but I didn't see the point since there was no one I wanted to dance with."

Dixie drew back. "Is that so?"

"Scout's honor," Aiden vowed.

"Were you a scout?" Dixie teased. "I didn't know that."

"I was the best, too," Aiden informed her, matter-of-factly. "But I don't want to brag or anything."

"Oh, of course not. Because telling me this isn't bragging," Dixie commented, dryly. "Modest, aren't ya?"

"Of course, I am," Aiden argued, puffing out his chest. His hands slid down to her waist, moving in time to the music, their bodies swaying gently. At that moment, they were caught in their own bubble, with nothing strong to penetrate.

And he wouldn't have it any other way.

Dixie shuddered, her arms reaching up, allowing her fingers to thread themselves through his hair. "Lucky me then."

"Very lucky," Aiden murmured, pressing his mouth to her ears. "Remember that party we me at?"

"You spilled your drink all over me and then demanded I apologize," Dixie recalled, amusement lacing her tone. "I remembered thinking you were the most arrogant man I'd ever met."

Aiden laughed. "I thought you were stuck up and spoiled."

"I guess we were both wrong," Dixie commented.

"I guess we were," Aiden agreed.

****

"Aiden," Dixie moaned, his name a quiet chant, falling from her lips as he pressed his lips to her neck, peppering it with light, open mouthed kisses, designed to drive her insane.

As predicted, she wrapped her around his shoulders and tilted her neck, allowing him better access. He kicked the door shut with the back of his leg, the sound echoing back to him in his apartment as he pressed her against the wall, his desire for her hanging over them like a thick and heavy cloud.

Her hands fell down to his waist, and circled his hips before one went around his neck, and the other on his chest, resting atop his thudding heart. It was beating at about a million miles minute, and he was certain she could feel it, thumping beneath her palms, but she didn't seem to care, as long in the moment as he was.

Soon enough, he pushed her blazer off her shoulders, letting it fall into a heap on the ground, joined by his own. His mouth traveled from her neck, down her collarbone and rested just atop her chest, delighted to see that it was rising and falling unevenly.

He had the same effect on her as she did on him, and the thought sent a thrill racing through him as he fumbled with the buttons on her shirt, cursing under his breath when they wouldn't come undone fast enough.

Finally, her breasts spilled forward, barely contained by her bra, and he cupped them, swallowing as he heard the sound of her heavy breathing accompanied by her little whimpers of encouragement.

Her hand moved from his chest, down the smattering of dark chest hair and came to rest just short of his happy trail, atop the line of his trousers. Without warning, she cupped him, pressing her fingers hard, making his eyes roll to the back of his head.

"God, I missed you, Dix." Aiden groaned, throwing his head back and letting out a deep grunt. She responded with her own moan as his fingers pushed past the fabric of her bra and flicked her sensitive nipples, turning them from a light rosy color to a vibrant red, as hard as pebbles.

His hands reached behind her back, and in one fluid movement, he unhooked the bra. She clasped her arms together, allowing it to slide forward and fall to the floor before she kicked it away and yanked his shirt over his head, pressing her upper half to his, skin on skin.

She felt hot to the touch, as if everywhere he went, a fire burned, raging out of control. Dixie jumped up and wrapped her legs around his waist, securing herself as his hands gripped her hips, his mouth hot and heavy atop hers.

Slowly, he moved backwards, in the general direction of his bedroom, wanting nothing more than to peel away every boundary between them till there was nothing left, and their bodies were intertwined.

Suddenly, he was at the foot of his bed, dropping Dixie onto the mattress. Immediately, she reached for him, her mouth hungry and scorching as she struggled with the zipper before she finally succeeded in pushing it down, and it fell to his ankles before he kicked it away, leaving him in nothing but her boxers.

In the next instant, he was sliding her pants down over thighs, taking his time as he watched her squirm and writhe, impatient for his touch. He pressed his lips to her neck, his tongue darting out to lick her skin, trailing a path down to her inner thighs, kissing around her core.

Dixie arched her back, her fingers digging into the sheets as she whispered his name, her dark eyes fixed on his. All the blood rushed to his groin as she yanked his boxers down and took him between her fingers, pumping hard.

Aiden used his teeth to pull down her underwear, lightly grazing the skin there, the smell of her washing over him, better than he remembered. In no time at all, they were both naked, a mass of limbs entangled, their heavy breathing filling the room.

As slowly as he could, Aiden nudged her legs open and slid into her, groaning as he went in all the way, filling her up. She stilled underneath him, her nails digging into his shoulders as she hissed, her eyes fluttering shut.

Ecstasy.

He kept his eyes on her, watching every expression flicker across her face as he moved, circling his hips before he eased out then thrust back in, the blood roaring in his ears as she gasped, pressing herself against him, the same urgent need pulsing through her.

This time, there was no hurry, no undercurrent of anger between them.

Instead, there was just the two of them, moving in harmony, and the sound of skin slapping against skin. He ran his fingers down from her ears all the way to the inside of her thighs and back up again, stopping atop her breasts.

He used both hands to squeeze them together, and Dixie moaned allowed, muttering under her breath as she bucked her hips, meeting each thrust with one of her own.

Taking as well as giving, unapologetically.

All too soon, she shouted, her body shaking with the force of her orgasm, ripping through her as she panted, sweat breaking out across her forehead. He braced his elbows on either side of the headboard and waited, enjoying that she was riding out her wave of pleasure.

Once she regained her breath, he began to thrust again, picking up the pace, a low growl forming in the back of his throat. Dixie rested her head in the crook of his neck, whispering in his ear, edging him on.

At last, he tumbled over the edge, his body wracked with tremors. Exhausted, he withdrew and collapsed next to her, and she curled into his side, running her fingers over his face.

Chapter 9
Dixie

She wanted to be happy.

After how hard she fought to make her dreams come true, leaving behind the only life she'd ever know, she figured she deserved to be. After all, she'd given up her chance at true love to make her father proud, and aside from a brief hint of nostalgia, she'd tried not to regret it.

Until now.

Seeing Aiden changed things, the electricity between them flaring up, especially with all the emotion hanging over them as they had sex. Unlike the first time which was charged with anger and frustration, the second time was different.

Full of nothing but healing and repairing old bridges.

In many ways, it was exactly how she imagined it would be after all those years spent away from him, reaching for him across her bed, a specter lying next to her in bed. The entire time was away, Dixie had tried to forget him, going above and beyond to exorcise him from her mind once and for all, but she had failed spectacularly.

Starting with the fact that she'd compared every single man she went out with Aiden, and they did fall short. Their eyes weren't the same shade, or their smile didn't reach their eyes.

Eventually, she'd come to the realization that she wasn't being fair to them, holding them up against an impossible standard, a pedestal even Aiden himself hadn't attained.

In reality, the memory of him had been strong, far too potent for her to overcome right away, so she'd given herself time, a wide berth of it to allow her heart to come to terms, grieving for what she could've been.

Yet, here she was.

Tangled up in Aiden once more and struggling to remind herself why she shouldn't. At the end of the day, Aiden had hurt her just as much as she hurt him, tit for tat, yet she couldn't seem to shake off his betrayal as easily as he had hers.

The truth of the matter was that when push came to shove, Aiden chose the coward's way out, opting to end things when shit starting getting real, and she hadn't forgiven him for it.

In fact, she wasn't even sure she *could*, and it *wasn't* for a lack of trying either. Since their heart to heart at the bar, she'd tried everything within her power to banish the anger, to get rid of it by telling herself that he didn't know the truth.

If he'd known, things would've turned out differently.

Hell, Aiden might've even gone with her to New York.

Aiden had believed he had the monopoly on all the pain and heartache, steadfastly sticking to his belief that she had betrayed him, choosing an opulent career over him.

In truth, it was Dixie who still carried the weight of her scars around, walking around with them pulsing an angry red, flaring up whenever she was close to Aiden who had no clue of the anguish inside her heart.

And how could he?

As far as he was concerned, she was the one who left him, but it was he who left first. By choosing not to fight for them, without even the entertaining the idea for a second, he'd dismissed her, tossing her aside as easily as an old pair of shoes he'd outgrown.

Yes, that was the problem, the root of it.

She couldn't seem to let herself be happy so long as the memory continued to tug on her, clamoring for her attention and holding up bright neon signs, a reminder of what he did. Without forgiveness, she'd be stuck, displaced in time, replaying that night over and over.

He left as well, Dixie. You're allowed to be mad at him for that. He's not the only one who gets to be angry.

No, he wasn't, but unlike Dixie, he seemed to have forgiven her, falling all over himself in his effort to make amends, to atone for a sin he hadn't even known, and she couldn't blame him for that.

A few days after their night together, she was finally ready to talk, to face their demons together and get the chance to air out her grievances, once and for all. Otherwise, they were doomed to repeat the same mistakes, and she didn't want to end up resenting Aiden.

Not when it was clear that her feelings for him had never gone away, were simply lying dormant, and waiting for the right moment to rear their head. Dixie gave a slight shake of her head and took a quick glance at her reflection in the glass window, grimacing at her serious frown.

Consciously, she made an effort to smooth it out, not wanting to look like she was taking him to court or something, with her brows furrowed together, and her lips pressed together.

You can do this, Dixie. You've got this. The worst is already over. He knows the truth now.

Knowing the truth had certainly changed things, shifted the rules a little. She ran her fingers along the outer edge of the mug and resisted the urge to look over at the clock hanging on the wall behind the counter.

Around her, people were scattered in various positions, clutching their coffee like it was their lifeline, their eyes glued to their screens. Hunched over in their chairs, they looked slightly comical, like zombies waiting to come back to life.

Her eyes slid over to the door, and her heart skipped a beat, doing an odd little lurch when she spotted Aiden's familiar head of hair. As if he sensed her across the café, his eyes found hers, and he offered a small smile, squeezing in between the throngs of people. He weaved in and out until he reached her, the smile on his face growing wider.

"Hey," Aiden greeted. "I was beginning to think that you were never going to call me back."

"I needed time to think," Dixie replied, eyes dropping to her drink. "Thanks for coming."

"Of course."

He slid into the seat across from her and signaled the waitressing, asking for a latte. Aiden leaned back into his seat, eyes flicking over the menu with disinterest before he set it down and clasped his hands in front of him.

Initially, she hadn't been sure he would agree to meet her, not after she'd practically scurried out of his apartment the last time they were together, hopping around the room, a Tasmanian devil, eager to get out of there before she did something stupid.

Like fall for him again.

She was in serious danger of unearthing every single thing that made her fall for him in the first place, so she'd panicked, pulling on the brakes before it could go any further and destroy her.

In all likelihood, she wouldn't survive him a second time, so she needed to be sure. With that in mind, she'd called him, and he'd agreed to cancel on his friend Julian in favor of meeting her for a cup of coffee, allowing her to choose the place, neutral territory.

"I'm sorry I ran out the other day," Dixie began, unable to meet his gaze as she fiddled with a packet of sugar, heart hammering against her ribcage. "I seem to be doing that a lot lately."

"Yeah, I've noticed," Aiden commented. The waitress set his mug down in front of him, and he curled his fingers around it, taking a quick sip before his eyes settled on hers, wide and expectant.

"I like you, Aiden," Dixie admitted. "And I know that sounds childish given that we're both adults now, and things are different now, but it's the truth, and it scares the crap out of me."

Aiden opened his mouth to say something, but she held up her hand, signaling for him to wait. She took a deep breath and held his gaze, counting backwards from ten.

"Actually, that's not true. I don't just like you. *I'm in love with you*, Aiden. I have been for seven *years*. I never *stopped* loving you, and there wasn't a day when we were apart that I didn't think about you, or wonder what you were doing."

More than that, she'd often considered crawling back to him on her hands and knees, begging for him to take her back, but the only thing that had stopped her was her pride, and the knowledge that if he'd truly wanted to, he would've shown up at her door, erasing any traces of doubt.

But the weeks had gone by, giving way to months, and all she got was silence.

"But I can't go through this with you again," Dixie added, quietly. "You gave up on me, Aiden. On us. When things got tough, you took the easy way out instead of staying and fighting, and I can't do that again."

As soon as the words left her lips, she leaned back in her seat, chest rising and falling unevenly, no longer carrying that burden, allowing it to unfurl its wings and soar, leaving her free and happy.

It had taken her five years to get here, but she'd finally done it, spoken her peace, and it felt damn good, as if she was weightless.

"You're right," Aiden admitted, abandoning his coffee altogether. "You're absolutely right, Dixie. I was young back then and stupid, and I thought that letting you go was the right decision for both of us."

"It wasn't," Dixie pointed out, not unkindly.

"I know that now, but I didn't know it back then. If I'd given myself a chance to think it over, I would've realized what a jackass I was. I never should've let you go, Dix."

A small kernel of hope blossomed within her heart, and she latched onto it, basking in its warmth. She'd imagined this over a thousand times in her head, playing back everything he'd say and do, but this was much better.

"I was only thinking of myself," Aiden continued, apologetically. "I can't change what I've done. I wish I could, but I'm not that person anymore."

She studied his expression, the slight tilt of his head, and realized that Aiden was still the man she fell in love with, but age had made him into a different person, altogether more mature and responsible.

In other words, it seemed as if he was now the man she wished he was all those years ago.

"If I had another chance, I wouldn't let you go," Aiden added, quietly. He reached for her hand across the table, intertwining their fingers.

Dixie wanted to believe him, but something was still stopping her, keeping her from throwing herself across the table and into his arms where she belonged.

"You're the only woman I've ever really loved, Dix, and the only want I want to be with. God knows you drive me crazy half the time, and you're a pain in my ass, but I wouldn't have it any other way."

Dixie choked back a laugh. "You're the one who is a pain in the ass. Who the hell drinks their hot chocolate with water instead of milk?"

"It's an acquired taste," Aiden defended, lips twitching in amusement.

Little by little, the ice around her heart began to thaw, and she covered his hands with hers, pressing a soft kiss on the inside of his wrist. "So, what do we do now?"

"What do you want to do?" Aiden asked. He released her hands, picked up her chair and set it down next to hers, so they were pressed against each other. "I want to be supportive of your dreams, Dix. I'm not making that mistake again. Do you want to go back to New York?"

Dixie hesitated. "I'm not sure. I don't mind life in New York, but I don't know if I'm really attached to it."

Aiden pressed a kiss to the side of her head. "How about we talk about this some more over lunch?"

Chapter 10
Aiden
Two years later

She crawled forward determinedly, her little limbs taking her as far her body would allow her even as she huffed and panted, frustrated with her lack of progress. As far as she was concerned, this was unacceptable.

Aiden chuckled as she headed towards the door and paused, staring up at it in, her eyebrows knitted together in confusion. It appeared she had met her match. Frustrated, she leaned back on her legs, opened her mouth and started babbling incoherently.

If he had to guess, he would say she was giving the door a piece of her mind, waving her fists up in the air, her lips puckered angrily. Tears of mirth ran down his face as he pushed himself up off the couch and scooped her up in his arms, giving her his thumb to chew in.

She shot him a long look before she sighed, resigned as she chewed on it, eyeing the door over his shoulders, an expression of fierce longing on her face. At one year old, Sophie Anderson Underwood was already a handful, a ball of energy, constantly on the move, and always looking for a flurry of activities to get involved in.

Dixie liked to call her a little firecracker, amused if slightly annoyed by her antics, alternating between wagging her fingers at her and giving her a stern talking to. Aiden, on the other hand, was completely besotted.

He had been since the day Julian's little girl opened her eyes, orbs of amber honey staring up at him in complete adoration. From that day on, he was wrapped around her finger, and everyone knew it; even Dixie liked to tease him about, muttering about how he was going to be her favorite uncle, no competition.

Not that he minded.

She fit perfectly against his chest, her head coming to rest in the crook of his neck, mumbling under her breath, an assortment of sounds he found to be quite adorable.

"You are regular Houdini, aren't you, Soph?" Aiden asked, setting her down in her playpen. Dressed in a yellow dress with small flowers printed on the side, and a bow in her hair, she looked every inch the hallmark child people advertised about.

But she was a lot more opinionated.

In a second, she yanked the bow out of her hair and threw it across the pen, crossing her arms over her chest when it landed harmlessly a few feet away, missing its mark entirely.

Based on what he was seeing, Aiden could already tell that she was going to be a stubborn girl, relentless in her pursuit of what she wanted, just like her mother. With her red hair and deep set eyes, she looked a like miniature version of Olive, and he couldn't help but adore her the more time he spent with her.

Aiden couldn't wait to have kids of his own.

Julian clapped him on the back, drawing his attention back to the present.

He turned to face his best man, monitoring Sophie out of the corner of his eye, and he hoped she wouldn't find a way to get out again. After all, she seemed to be coming up with new and inventive ways to do that, so he couldn't decide if he was proud or angry.

Julian frowned as he eyed Aiden's tie disapprovingly. "What did you do? I just fixed this."

"I hate ties," Aiden complained. "They remind me of collars, like I'm in prison or something."

Julian rolled his eyes. "You're being dramatic. Besides, consider yourself lucky. It takes us an hour at most to get ready. Do you have any idea how long it takes the woman?"

Aiden shuddered at the thought, imagining hours of being cooped up in a room while people poked and prodded, going every inch of available skin to make sure she was perfect and presentable.

Personally, Aiden didn't see the point, but it wasn't his call to make.

All he really wanted was for Julian to be his best man, and for his daughter, Sophie, to be his flower girl.

"I don't want to picture that," Aiden decided, straightening his back and allowing Julian to adjust his tie.

"I wouldn't either," Julian agreed. "It's almost time, man."

"Got any last words of wisdom to impart upon me?" Aiden joked, moving away from the mirror and leaning over the play pen. Julian mirrored his position, his expression thoughtful.

"I'm not sure," Julian answered. "I mean, our arrangement isn't exactly normal, you know, but I guess just remember, whenever you're fighting that you're on the same side, and learn to let the small things go."

"That sounds like good advice," Aiden commented, offering his best friend a small smile. "I hope I remember that."

Julian squeezed his shoulder. "You will."

In the back of his mind, he wondered what Dixie was doing, and if she felt the swarm of butterflies beat mercilessly against her stomach, demanding to be acknowledged. In all likelihood, she was cursing the fact that he managed to convince her to have a wedding to begin with.

Yes, unlike most women, Dixie hadn't dreamt of a big white wedding, envisioning all the details down to the flowers. On the contrary, she'd just wanted to elope, make an appointment at the courthouse and get it over with.

However, Aiden had put his foot down, insisting on at least having an event where they could invite the important people in their life. On a day like today, it was important to be surrounded by love and laughter.

In that one instance, it appeared their roles were reversed, and they'd had long and extensive conversations about the topic, beating it to death till they finally reached a compromise.

The courthouse had a garden, a small wrap around garden with pots of flowers tended to do by well-wishers, and lush green grass. Granted, it wasn't exactly what Aiden had in mind, but he'd known that the key to getting through it was compromise.

As was the case with most decisions in a relationship.

At the end of the day, as long as he got to marry Dixie, to call her his wife and stand by her side for the rest of their days then he didn't care if they were getting married in a graveyard.

Though thankfully that wasn't the case.

Eventually, Aiden put his hand on the knob and slid the door open, poking his head out to see what was happening. From his vantage point, he could hardly see a thing except for the long and narrow corridor with flickering florescent lights.

At the end of it all was the room they'd agreed to vacate for Dixie's benefit. A smattering of giggles broke out, and his face broke out into a grin, imagining her walking toward him, a shared look passing between them before they paid attention to anyone else.

"Getting cold feet?" Julian teased, clapping Aiden on the back. "That's okay too, man. Listen, I know I wasn't supportive in the beginning, but as long as Dixie makes you happy, that's all that matters, and I can see she does."

"She does," Aiden agreed, craning his neck to give Julian a long look over his shoulder. "I don't remember you being this nervous at your wedding."

It was true.

Then again, Julian was never the type of guy to get hung up on the details, or worry about things he couldn't control. In fact, Aiden remembered him standing at the altar, completely at ease in his tux.

Julian chuckled. "Trust me, I was, but I was just good at hiding it."

Aiden raised an eyebrow. "Too good. Your poker face is shit, so I don't know how you pulled it off."

Julian paused. "Honestly? When I saw Olive headed towards me, I didn't need to pretend. I just knew. It'll be the same for you."

Aiden leaned back and offered Julian a small smile. "Thanks, man."

"I'm going to take Sophie to Olive, and I'll see you out there, okay?" Julian brushed imaginary lint off of his jacket and stood up straight. "I'll sneak you something strong later if you need it."

Aiden shoved Julian playfully, giving him a mock serious look. "I don't want to be drunk during my wedding."

"Not yet," Julian pointed out. "You might change your mind, and I'll be there if you do."

Aiden shook his head, lips twitching in amusement. "I just want to get it over with."

Julian nodded, bent down to scoop Sophie into his arms and planted a kiss atop her head, ruffling her hair in the process. She shot her father a brief look, mildly annoyed at the interruption, before she turned her attention back to babbling.

As soon as Julian was gone, Aiden was left alone with his thoughts.

Outside, the opening notes of the music began to play. Aiden coughed and straightened his back. He swung the door open and strode out, shoving his nerves to the back of his mind.

Before long, Aiden was standing under the arch, his hands shoved deep into his pockets as he waited for Dixie to emerge. People shifted in their seats on both sides of the aisle, sweat forming on their foreheads.

He resisted the urge to check on his watch, wondering what was taking so long when a familiar head of hair rounded the corner, knocking the breath right out of him. Aiden sucked in a harsh breath, his heart picking up the pace till it was practically ready to leap out of his chest and onto the grass.

Her eyes found his across the way, and she kept her gaze fixed on him, a slight smile hovering on the edge of her lips. She glided towards him, the train of her dress swishing behind her.

When she finally reached him, he was overcome with the desire to scoop her into his arms and press a deep kiss to her lips, until the rest of the room, and its occupants melted away.

Instead, he held his arm out, she tucked her hand into the crook of his elbow, and they climbed up the smell set of stairs, waiting for the minister to start. Overhead, the sun shone down on them, with no clouds as far as they eye could see.

In the first row, Sophie sat, balanced on Olive's hip, with Julian and Milo on either side smiling and waving at them. Dixie blew her a quick kiss before she turned her attention to the minister and recited her vows, her eyes glazing over.

No sooner had the priest announced as man and wife than Aiden swept her into his arms, his lips descending against hers. She responded by wrapping her arms around him and smiling into the kiss.

Around them, a chorus of applause went up, polite at first then lowered as some of the guys in the back hooted and hollered. Eventually, they pulled away and rested their foreheads against each other, slightly out of breath.

"I've been wanting to do that all day," Aiden admitted, pressing his lips to her forehead. "Mrs. Lawson."

"I said I would consider taking your last time," Dixie teased.

"What about a hyphen? Aricello-Lawson?"

Dixie made a face as he spun her out on the dance floor before he spun her back in. "That sounds like cough medicine, and not the nice fruity kind."

"Lawson Aricello?" Aiden suggested, chuckling when she shot him a dirty look.

"Our last names just don't work together," Dixie admitted.

"That's okay," Aiden assured her. "Because we do."

"Look at you going all cheesy on me," Dixie teased. "Don't go all sentimental on me, Lawson."

"I wouldn't dream of it, Aricello."

Made in United States
North Haven, CT
31 December 2023

46896120R00026